THE LITTLE GUYS

VERA BROSGOL

Roaring Brook Press
New York

For Omar

Copyright © 2019 by Vera Brosgol

Published by Roaring Brook Press
Roaring Brook Press is a division of Holtzbrinck
Publishing Holdings Limited Partnership
175 Fifth Avenue, New York, NY 10010
mackids.com

Library of Congress Control Number: 2018944876

ISBN: 978-1-62672-442-6

Our books may be purchased in bulk for promotional, educational, or business use. Please contact your local bookseller or the
Macmillan Corporate and Premium Sales Department at (800) 221-7945 ext. 5442 or by e-mail at MacmillanSpecialMarkets@macmillan.com.

First edition, 2019
Book design by Andrew Arnold
Printed in China by Hung Hing Off-set Printing Co. Ltd., Heshan City, Guangdong Province

This book was drawn with dip pen and acrylic ink and painted in watercolor, with some Adobe Photoshop shenanigans afterwards.

10 9 8 7 6 5 4 3 2 1

You are looking at the
strongest guys in the whole forest.

Down here.

On this island.

We are the Little Guys.

Yes, we are small. But there are a lot of us.

Together we are strong, and we can get all we need.

We can cross deep water where
you can't see the bottom.

Off to find breakfast for the Little Guys.

We never get lost in the big, dark forest.

Nothing to fear for the Little Guys.

We can find enough food for all of us.

A piece of cake for the Little Guys.

We can lift things that weigh more than we do.

No sweat for the Little Guys.

We can climb the
tallest tree there is.

Easy peasy for the Little Guys!

We can dig through anything that stands in our way!

Nothing stops the Little Guys!

We can beat up
the biggest animal
we find!

Don't mess with the Little Guys!

Together we are strong,
and we have . . .

everything . . . ?

We . . .

have . . .

every . . .

thing . . .

We are the Little Guys.

Yes, there are a lot of us.

But we are small.

We have all we need,

and together . . .

. . . we are strong.